Clara Vulliamy

THE BIRTHDAY SURPRISE

Dotty
DETECTIVE

HarperCollins *Children's Books*

First published in Great Britain by HarperCollins
Children's Books in 2018
HarperCollins *Children's Books*
is a division of HarperCollins*Publishers* Ltd,
1 London Bridge Street, London, SE1 9GF

HarperCollins*Publishers*
Macken House, 39/40 Mayor Street Upper
Dublin 1, D01 C9W8, Ireland

The HarperCollins website address is: www.harpercollins.co.uk

16

Text and illustrations © Clara Vulliamy 2018

ISBN 978-0-00-824841-3

Clara Vulliamy asserts the moral right to be identified as the
author and illustrator of the work.

Printed and bound by CPI Group (UK) Ltd, Croydon, CR0 4YY

This book is produced from independently certified FSC™ paper
to ensure responsible forest management.

For more information visit: www.harpercollins.co.uk/green

For Melanie, Eva and Claudia,
with much love

Read the whole series:

**This book
belongs to . . .**

DOT

and McClusky

SUNDAY

This is me – Dot!

I live with Mum, the twins (my brother and sister, Alf and Maisy) and my **crazy** dog, McClusky.

It's **noodles** for tea, which is my *absolute* favourite, but I can hardly concentrate . . .

doodles
of
noodles

because I am too *utterly totally incredibly* **MASSIVELY** excited . . .

9

My birthday is in exactly TWO WEEKS! And tonight I'm making my **party invitations**.

The twins' birthday is in August and for their last party we had a picnic in the park with ice lollies and a machine that **blows bubbles**.

We don't know when McClusky's birthday is because he's a rescue dog,

so each year
he has THREE
birthday parties
(just in
case he didn't
have enough
special celebrations
before he became
part of our
family).

But when it comes to MY party I am *completely* in the dark. Mum refuses to tell me anything about what she is planning.

Even when I say, "**Please, please, PLEASE** – just give me ONE tiny clue!" she does the zip-the-lips gesture.

"My lips are sealed," she says.

Bedtime. This might look like just an ordinary bedroom, but OH NO.

I have something EXTREMELY important to tell you …

Me, my best friend – Beans – and McClusky are super-secret, super-sleuthing DETECTIVES!

JOIN THE DOTS DETECTIVES

13

And my bedroom is our HQ.

This is where we study the clues and piece together the evidence. However murky the mystery or fiendishly tricky the puzzle, together we always solve the case.

??

But at the moment the **biggest** mystery in my life is – what will my birthday party be?

Roller-disco? Go-karting? Will there be a magician?

I make party invitations for all my friends with my **awesome** stationery collection.

Woo-HOOO! I can use my new clock stamp to show the times!

I'm pretty pleased with the result...

WOO-HOOO! YOU ARE INVITED TO DOT'S PARTY! SUNDAY 11TH MARCH TO

MONDAY

Mum is calling,

"HURRY UP! WE'RE GOING TO BE LATE FOR SCHOOL!"

I'm already standing by the front door ready to leave, but the twins are charging up and down the hall,

wearing their school jumpers
like capes and pretending
to be

SUPERHEROES.

They ALWAYS make us need to rush.

Arriving at school there is only JUST time to say hello to the **school-gate gang**, McClusky's dog friends.

They wait together outside school at dropping-off and going-home time, because they aren't allowed into the playground.

I reach up to pat big Geoffrey, and reach down to stroke little *sausage dog puppy*, Chipolata.
Her ears are SO SOFT.

Hurrying over to line up and hand out my party invitations and – oh! – there's a NEW BOY I've never seen before.

At registration, our teacher, Mr Dickens, says, "Listen up, everybody! Let's all give a HUGE, friendly welcome to Bradley, who has just joined our class!"

We all call out, **"HI!"** **"HEY!"** **"YAY!"** **"HOLA!"** **"HOWDY!"** until Frankie gets carried away with this huge, friendly welcome and falls off his chair.

"Tell us a bit about yourself, Bradley," says Mr D.

"Well, for a start, I am good at **LOTS** of things!" says Bradley. He shows us his achievement badges – football captain, school council, spelling bee award, outstanding pupil . . .

They are all bright red, the colour of his old school, not our school colours, which are yellow and blue.

Bradley sits on the table next to ours, right behind Beans.

Me and Beans are chatting about my **party mystery**. I see Bradley watching us.

I'm just in the middle of my list of guesses, but Bradley **interrupts** by *tapping* Beans on the shoulder and starts talking to him.

While we are meant to be sorting out the pen pots, Bradley wants to show Beans his shiny red *STAR PUPIL* pencil case. Beans is very impressed.

I remember being the new person in class and not knowing anyone at first, so I try not to mind.

And now Mr D is saying, "I have an *announcement!*" and doing his

exciting news dance.

"Today we will start our Ancient Egypt project! There will be loads of fun stuff like a trip to the museum and a big art display in the hall for the rest of the school to admire... and next Friday will be

EGYPT DAY

when we will all dress up – which will be extra special because it is also the same day as MY BIRTHDAY!"

Amazing!

TWO birthdays only two days apart – mine and Mr D's!

Now Mr D is drawing **balloons** and birthday cakes around the date of his birthday on the classroom wall calendar.

FRIDAY
9th

When Mr D is happy, he makes up silly songs.

"I can hardly wait! It will be so great! Hip hip hip hoorays! Counting down the days!" he sings.

He is easily as **excited** about his birthday as I am about mine – which is *so funny* because he is a grown-up!

Breaktime. Beans goes off with
Bradley, but that's fine as I am busy
eating my Cheesy Wheat Crunchers
and having a

brilliant

idea . . .

In class while Mr D is distracted in the stationery cupboard, I whisper my idea to my friends ...

"Let's do something *really special* for Mr D's birthday," I say, "and make a lovely surprise present for him!" They think this is GREAT!

We all do secret **high fives** under the table.

"I'm **too excited** to wait – I'll start making it tonight!" I tell them. "Everyone, bring in your best *stickers* and **glitter** and **decorations** tomorrow!"

30

In Geography we are drawing maps
of **Ancient Egypt** for the class
display in the hall.

Beans, who is *brilliant* at maps, is in a
pair with Bradley.

Me and Fiyaz do our best with some yellow and blue pencils. The Red Sea looks like a **weird** rabbit and our camels are a *bit* funny, so we mainly draw lots of sand dunes instead.

Back at home, *super-speedily* having my tea so I can rush to Dot HQ . . .

I think I have the PERFECT thing for Mr D's special present!

Rummaging in my shoebox of extra-precious treasures...

Here it is - a photo from our school trip
to **ADVENTURE**

CAMP.

We are all in it - me, Beans, Amy, Joe, Fiyaz, Frankie, Nadia and Kirstie - and Mr D is in the middle with a huge smile on his face. I make a card frame for it, and decorate around the edge with glittery pens, pom-poms and birthday stickers.

*He is going to absolutely **LOVE** it!*

Tuesday

Rushing to line up with Mr D's present safely in my bag ... Beans is already here, chatting to Bradley.

Beans is showing him his shiny new **ten-sided dice**. I REALLY want to see too, but Bradley turns his back on me so my view is blocked.

It takes AGES to find a good moment to show everyone Mr D's present ...

But at breaktime it's wet play, which is REALLY LUCKY! While Mr D is distracted by dunking a digestive biscuit into his tea and trying to fish it out again ...

I secretly show my group of friends the photo in the collaged frame.

All together we add the extra decorations brought in from home. Joe has **sparkly rainbow glitter**, Nadia has brought in tiny **pearl buttons** and Fiyaz has filled his pocket with different coloured **sequins**.

It's looking

AMAZING!

Beans joins in with some pieces
of nice stripy string he finds at
the bottom of his bag. But Bradley
makes a sulky face so Beans goes
off to sit with him instead.

In Maths we are making a sugar-lump
pyramid for the **EGYPT** display.

This is how we do it . . .

4 rows of 12 sugar lumps
arranged in a square...

then 4 rows of 11 sugar lumps stepped in slightly and glued into place...

the same with 4 rows of 10

and repeat until there is just one on the top!

Mr D tells us about the pharaoh's burial chambers, and the **SECRETS OF THE GREAT PYRAMIDS**.

"Imagine – caskets of treasure hidden behind **locked** doors along cramped, dusty corridors, undiscovered for

THOUSANDS

of

years!"

he says.

At going-home time we put the finishing touches to Mr D's special surprise present, and Joe adds one last handful of **glitter** for extra sparkle.

We all write birthday messages on the back.

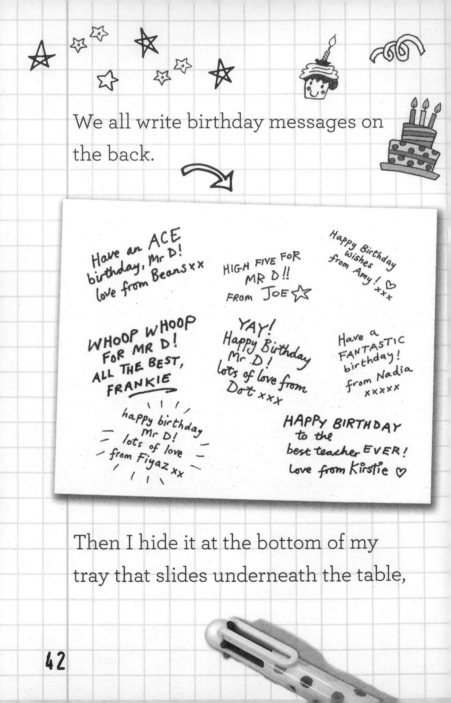

Have an ACE birthday, Mr D! love from Beans xx

HIGH FIVE FOR MR D!! FROM JOE ☆

Happy Birthday wishes from Amy! ♡ xxx

WHOOP WHOOP FOR MR D! ALL THE BEST, FRANKIE

YAY! Happy Birthday Mr D! lots of love from Dot xxx

Have a FANTASTIC birthday! from Nadia xxxxx

happy birthday Mr D! lots of love from Fiyaz xx

HAPPY BIRTHDAY to the best teacher EVER! love from Kirstie ♡

Then I hide it at the bottom of my tray that slides underneath the table,

buried under a pile of things that I
keep there.

At home, clearing the dishes after
tea and feeling really happy ... This
is going to be an EXTRA-good
evening!

Cosy on the sofa under my best polka-dot blanket, mug of hot chocolate, watching my favourite TV programme EVER, which is **FRED FANTASTIC - ACE DETECTIVE**.

There are many **dastardly** villains on the mean streets of the big city, up to no good. It's down to detectives Fred and his cool sidekick, Flo, to put a stop to them.

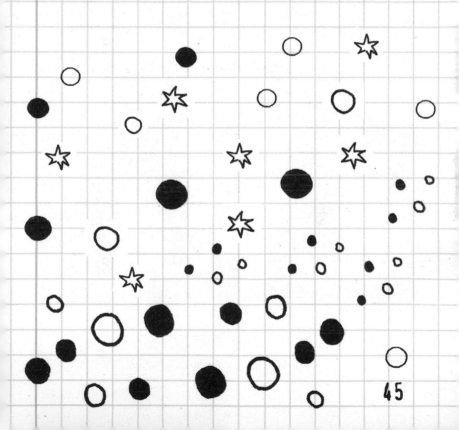

And now that Mr D's present is finished *PHEW* I can concentrate on writing *my own* birthday-present list!

red trainers

glow-in-the-dark paperclips

dotty stickers

Fred and Flo's Fantastically Fab Storybook

dotty socks

change-colour umbrella

Pony

Wednesday

Coming into class at registration,
I just want to **admire** Mr D's present
again. Rummaging down to the
bottom of my tray ...

I CAN'T SEE IT!

Frantically searching again ...
The special present
has

DISAPPEARED.

This is a

DISASTER!

I MUST find it before anyone else
realises it's gone and starts a *panic*.

While everyone bustles to and fro
to move places for English, I secretly
peep inside the other trays at my
table. Could it have been moved *by
mistake?*

Beans keeps a **huge** collection of elastic bands in his tray, Frankie has a *very old* apple core and lots of important unopened school letters he never took home and Amy has the neatest, tidiest tray I have EVER seen...

But NO – no sign of Mr D's present.

Everyone is heading out into the playground for breaktime. Now's my chance for a bigger search! I pretend I've forgotten my water bottle and *hurry* back to the classroom.

I check the stationery cupboard,
    the lunchbox crates,
        the shelves . . .
            but

NO SIGN.

At lunchtime I'm feeling **too stressed** to eat more than *one bite* of my sandwich . . .

and even **more stressed** when everyone starts asking me about my party!

"What sort of party will it be?" asks Kirstie.

"Tell us, Dot!" says Fiyaz.

"It's a **SECRET!**" I say. "I am keeping it
UNDER MY HAT."

I smile *mysteriously* and just hope that
nobody guesses I have no idea!

Usually I would talk to Beans about
this, but he is sitting at a different
table, eating his lunch with Bradley.

To make matters EVEN WORSE, Laura
(who is *not* always my favourite
person, I can tell you) starts talking
about all the amazing super-fancy
parties she has had.

"Once loads of us went to the theatre and the tickets were *really* expensive and afterwards we went to the BEST restaurant. And another time I had a **spa pamper party** and we put our feet in a bucket of cucumber and—"

But I've stopped listening. This is making me feel uneasy. I'm pretty sure that putting my feet in a bucket of cucumber ISN'T my idea of the perfect party, but I wish I DID know what Mum is planning!

At going-home time when everyone is distracted by packing their bags, I search around the coat pegs . . . but NOTHING.

Lying on my bed, thinking about
Mr D's missing present ...

And worrying.

There's no avoiding it: I must tell the
others in the morning.

Thursday

As soon as we get into the classroom, I beckon my friends into a huddle and whisper, "It's *gone* – Mr D's special present is **MISSING!**"

They GASP in *horror*.

"EXTREMELY *mysterious!*" says Beans, catching my eye. I know *exactly* what he is thinking – this is just the kind of **puzzle** me and Beans are so good at solving!

"Have you searched everywhere?" asks Amy.

"High and low?" adds Joe.

"I have looked EVERYWHERE I can think of ..." I tell them.

"A-HA!" says a voice behind us. It's Bradley – he has been eavesdropping and heard everything! "You may have looked everywhere *you* can think of," he says, "but it will take a **brilliant** detective like ME to find it!"

Me and Beans look at each other in utter bewilderment. Together we have secretly solved the **trickiest** cases and the MURKIEST OF MYSTERIES. And now Bradley reckons HE is a detective too!

I realise Bradley is watching. I am just about to say something to Beans, but Bradley interrupts.

"I know," he says, "let's make it a boys-against-girls detective race to find the present – and see who finds it first. I bet the BOYS will win!"

I can see Beans hesitating, but Bradley bossily rounds up his team. So I gather mine together too.

The girls' team is Kirstie, me, Amy and Nadia. The boys' team is Joe, Frankie, Bradley, Beans and Fiyaz.

THE CASE OF THE MISSING BIRTHDAY PRESENT has begun – and it's *Girl Detectives versus Boy Detectives*!

"This case will be a piece
of cake – SO EASY!"
Bradley says to his team.

"We need to keep searching, and look
for clues . . ." I say to my team.

We look again in all the same places.
I might have missed something . . .
BUT NO LUCK.

"Maybe it wasn't *accidentally* lost?"
I say. It's all starting to look very
suspicious...

We are just heading over to the
library when Bradley says,
"Dot, YOU must have deliberately
hidden the present *yourself*!"
He is pointing triumphantly.
"You have glitter on your
hands! LOOK!"

It's true, I do, BUT …

"So do YOU, Bradley!" I say.

Kirstie adds, "And what about Joe?
He even has glitter in his HAIR!"

We are ALL a bit **glittery!** Ever since
Joe brought in his rainbow glitter, it
has gone pretty much everywhere.
So the glitter *isn't* a clue after all.

We hurry over to the furthest bookshelves to choose our books, but *really* we are discussing the case. "We need to think about **SUSPECTS**," I say.

"Who could have got into the classroom before school starts in the morning?" Nadia wonders.

"I know!" says Amy. "It must be someone in the **Breakfast Club!**

But WHO?"

"Ace detective work, team!" I say.
"We MUST get a look at the
Breakfast Club list . . ."

Back in class we saunter *extremely casually* past Mr D's desk, but the clubs book is closed. Mr D raises an eyebrow at us.

Heading out to lunch, I see the book is **open**! This could be my chance!

I saunter backwards past Mr D's desk ... but

AAARGH

it's open on the Chess Club page!

Mr D raises the other eyebrow.

In the afternoon we are learning about hieroglyphs, which is **Ancient Egyptian** picture writing.

Interesting fact – a hieroglyphic word can be written **right to left** *or* **left to right**. You can tell which way it should be read because the humans or animals *always* face towards the beginning of the word.

We practise writing our names.
I write McClusky's name too – but backwards!

At going-home time, the clubs book
is open on the right page.

AT LAST

I see the Breakfast Club list . . .

In the chaos of the playground, I
can't find Nadia, Amy or Kirstie to
tell them about my discovery.

Back at home, I finish my spaghetti
hoops *super-speedily*, and rush to
Dot HQ . . .

*I write a note to the rest of the girls'
team using hieroglyphs.*

Laura

must be up to her

old tricks

AGAIN!

FRIDAY

I carefully hide my hieroglyph note inside my library book before we set off on the walk to school.

In class, hanging up my coat and unpacking my bag, I'm waiting for the right moment to secretly slip the note to the other girl detectives . . .

But – **DISASTER** – the note
falls out of my book onto the floor
and –

EEEeeeeK

– without realising
Frankie steps on it and it is
STUCK TO HIS SHOE!!

Frankie walks over to his place and I
hurry after him. But just as I reach
down to grab the note . . .

Fiyaz picks it up, folds it into a paper
aeroplane and sends it –

WHEEEEE!

– across the room
and it is caught – OH NO! –
by Bradley!

He puts it in his pocket.

DRAT!

NO CHANCE to speak to Amy, Nadia or Kirstie *all morning* – Bradley is hovering nearby all the time!

Usually I go to Knitting Club with Beans at Friday lunchtime, but I haven't seen him much this week so I don't think I will go today.

After lunch, we go over to the ICT suite to research facts about a desert animal. I choose a jerboa – they are so cute and h○p like a tiny *kangaroo*!

long ears like a rabbit

nocturnal

long tail for balancing

long back legs for running (can run up to 24 km an hour!)

I am sitting next to Laura which is an unexpected opportunity to investigate **THE MAIN SUSPECT!**

"So, Laura," I ask in a casual, roundabout way, "what sort of things do you eat at Breakfast Club?"

"Oh, I haven't been to Breakfast Club for WEEKS – I have been practising violin at home before school instead. My violin exam is very soon – I shall definitely do **brilliantly!**"

So it couldn't have been Laura after all. It was a *red herring*, which isn't anything to do with fish – it means that this clue led us down the wrong path.

I finish my jerboa facts, and wonder what our next move should be.

Bradley leans back in his chair and puts his hands behind his head.

"I'm feeling **GOOD** about **solving** this case *very soon!*"

"Bradley is a *really* good detective!" Beans says to me.

I don't say anything. After all the cases me and Beans have solved together, this makes me feel a bit sad.

At going-home time, Mr D gives out letters reminding us about the museum trip on Monday, and asking if we have any dolls at home we no longer want ... "AND don't forget it's dressing up for **EGYPT DAY** next Friday!" he says. "Have a fab weekend, everybody!"

Saturday

We take McClusky for a walk in the park even though it's raining.

I think about the case while we splash through puddles – thank goodness I am wearing my dotty boots!

Bradley seems so sure he will find the missing present first. What does the boys' team know

THAT WE DON'T?

On the way home, Mum asks, "Shall we call by at Beans's house? See if he would like to come over?"

Since Bradley arrived at our school, Beans hasn't had much time for me. Would he *even want* to come over?

"Not today, thanks, Mum," I say.

After lunch, to distract myself from worrying about the case, I think about my birthday instead.

ONLY EIGHT DAYS TO GO!

I design my **ideal birthday cake**. It is pink sponge with white icing, and I can't decide between sugar beans or jazzies so I add BOTH. On top there are four upside-down

ice-cream cones with little flags
flying. It looks like a **crazy** dotty
castle!

I put the drawing up on the fridge
with my biggest and best magnet
so Mum will notice it.

I try to find out more from Mum
about my party too, but she seems
to have forgotten all about it! "What
party?" she says. "Oh, *that* party..."

Now this is WORRYING TOO. Will
it be a **big** flop?

Sunday

Mum says she is **VERY BUSY** this morning and asks if we can help with some household chores in the kitchen.

I sort the paper in the recycling box and the twins have a go with the dustpan and brush. Alf holds the dustpan and Maisy brushes, but they don't *quite* have the knack ...

there is a trail of **Doggylicious** dog-biscuit crumbs

EVERYWHERE!

Mum takes McClusky into her room.

When he comes back, he is VERY excited and I glimpse a piece of gold thread on his ear.

WHAT

IS

GOING

ON?

Today it's the museum trip! Mum
gives me some spending money for
the shop, and I put it carefully in my
panda purse.

Straight away after registration it's
time to set off. I am in a pair with Joe
to walk to the museum. Bradley and
Beans are walking behind us.

"I'm really looking forward to your
party!" says Joe. "I LOVE birthdays."

"Are you inviting BOYS as well
as girls to your party, Dot?" says
Bradley. "Girls' parties are STUPID."

"*Of course* boys are invited to my
party!" I say. "Why wouldn't they
be?"

Bradley *scowls*. Does he think that boys hanging out with girls is mixing with the enemy?

CRAZY!

In the museum we learn all about the different **EGYPTIAN GODS**.

HORUS   ANUBIS   THOTH   ISIS

We see a REAL mummy in an open sarcophagus, which is a stone coffin from **ancient times**, and a turquoise statue of a hippopotamus, and we even see a

MUMMIFIED CAT!!!

We all love the grisly facts about mummification.

Actually not *quite* all – Laura, who is squeamish, hurries past the jar with a baboon head on top and mummified lungs inside.

There's also a **brilliant** model showing the inside of a pyramid, with

secret passages and **hiding places**.

Eating our packed lunches, Mr D says, "Today should be giving you loads of good ideas for your **Egyptian costumes** on Friday!"

EEK!

I haven't thought of **anything** yet!

I **love** dressing up.

Once, me and Beans went to a
fancy-dress party as a

TWO-HEADED MONSTER

in one of my mum's big coats.

I look over and see Beans and
Bradley pretending to be mummies
and

collapsing into giggles.

I miss Beans.

It's going-home time when we arrive
back at school. In fact, Mum is already
in the playground waiting for me.

The girls' detective team hasn't had
any chance to work on the case today.
We MUST make up for lost time
tomorrow!

For tea we make **funny-face** baked potatoes. Mine has cucumber and peas for eyes, tomato for the nose and mouth, and cress for the hair!

TUESdAy

Mr D is talking excitedly about his birthday. "I can hardly sleep!" he says.

This makes me and the girls' team worry *even more* about his missing present.

"Fingers crossed for a LUCKY BREAK in the case today!" I say.

"Have you ever wondered what the **Ancient Egyptians** did for their birthdays?" Mr D carries on.

"The pharaoh in **3000 BC** had the *first ever* mentioned birthday party in history. But it was the ANCIENT GREEKS who first put *candles* on birthday cakes!"

In Art we each make a **sarcophagus** out of card and decorate them with **Egyptian patterns.**

We take our **sarcophagi** over to the hall to add to the display. I'm just putting mine in a good position when I notice something…

That's odd. What's a tiny **pearl button** doing here? I pop it in my pocket.

We are heading outside for break time. Bradley, who has gone out first, says *very loudly*

"LOOK!"

He is pointing **dramatically** towards a *small trail* of sequins leading across the playground.

He is acting like a **GREAT** detective, studying the sequins, staring into the distance and then *writing something* in his notebook.

The other boys are standing around not doing much. I have noticed that Bradley doesn't **share** a lot with his team.

I *speedily* gather the girls' team into a huddle. "The missing present must have been hidden somewhere OUTSIDE!" I say.

"Let's split up into twos," says Kirstie.

"That way, we can cover more ground."

We search **every corner** of the playground . . .

And again at lunchtime . . . But it leads to

nothing.

Another **dead end**.

Arriving home, the first thing I see when I walk in through the front door is a huge **MYSTERIOUS** object under a sheet. There is a sign taped to it in Mum's writing.

This is *extremely* puzzling!

After tea I watch a **FRED FANTASTIC** episode in which Fred is struggling to solve a case without Flo.

It makes me think about the

Case of the Missing Birthday Present . . .

I have a BRILLIANT team, but I'm finding this mystery *so much trickier* without Beans on my side too – he would know what to do next.

This girls-against-boys thing is

SILLY.

Me and Beans – like Fred and Flo – are a **very cool team** and always work best together!

WEDNESDAY

Today we are using the unwanted dolls brought in from home to make our mummies!

They are a **STRANGE** selection.

Frankie has brought in Cynthia and tells us, "I used to take her *everywhere* when I was little until both her eyes fell out and one leg fell off – now she's *Cynthia the zombie doll!*"

Bradley says, "UGH! What **BOYS** have **DOLLS?**" and laughs. Beans laughs too.

Beans has been acting differently since Bradley arrived.

Usually on Wednesday morning me and Beans talk about last night's episode of **FRED FANTASTIC** because he loves it too, but I don't think I want to today.

We are cutting lengths of bandage to wrap round our mummies. This gives me a **brilliant** idea for a new way to send a message – **MUMMY MAIL!**

When no one is looking, I write a **loooooong** message to the other girl detectives on the back of a piece of bandage . . .

ONLY TWO DAYS LEFT! WHERE IS THE PRESENT?

But

DISASTER!

My message is *scooped up* with the other pieces of bandage, and too soon it is wrapped round a mummy and glued into place before they can read it.

WHO IS HIDING IT ???

AGAIN I cannot get a message to the rest of my team!

To make matters worse, Bradley is always teasing us. "You seem to be getting NOWHERE!" he says. "But *I* have discovered a **VERY** important clue."

He makes a big show of writing in his notebook.

I am SO worried. Mr D's present is still missing – the whole thing was my idea and it all feels like my fault. And it's too late to find something else to give him.

We have tied ourselves up in knots. Fred Fantastic says this a lot. It doesn't mean you are actually really knotted …

It means you are very confused about a worrying problem.

McClusky comes in. He can always tell if I need comforting. He brings his chewed squeaky-bone toy and drops it into my lap.

"No, McClusky. I can't give that to Mr D instead …"

And nothing seems to be happening about my party.

Has Mum forgotten?

Thursday

Lining up in the playground to go into class, Bradley is talking loudly to the other boy detectives.

"I am following a **very important lead** and we shall *definitely* find the present TOMORROW!"
The others cheer and

punch the air
triumphantly.

In class we are putting the finishing touches to our **Ancient Egypt** display. Mr D brings something out of his desk that we weren't expecting: a small toy robot!

He tells us that a robot with a camera was sent into the Great Pyramid, along undiscovered corridors, to explore *unknown hidden chambers.*

I think about the secret hiding places inside the pyramids ...

And, while I'm thinking, I'm absent-mindedly twiddling the tiny pearl button in my pocket that I picked up in the hall ...

Why hadn't I thought of this before? It must be one of the buttons Nadia brought in for Mr D's birthday present! What was it doing in the **Egypt** display?

The penny drops ...

I have a

EUREKA MOMENT!

As soon as the bell goes for breaktime, Amy, Nadia and Kirstie disappear to Choir practice but I RUSH across to the hall.

I lift the sugar-lump pyramid – and there, inside, is Mr D's **missing birthday present!**

And what's this? Half hidden underneath I see a FOOTBALL CAPTAIN badge. It must have fallen off the culprit's jumper! But a RED badge, not yellow and blue!

It was **BRADLEY** who **hid the present!**

I pop the present under my jumper for safekeeping and hurry out into the playground to wait for the other girl detectives, so I can tell them what has happened.

"Bradley has known all along where it was because *he* put it there!" I say. "When he said I had **glittery** hands, he was trying to **distract us** by

BLAMING ME!"

"He must have planted the sequins as a false trail to send us in the wrong direction!" says Kirstie.

"It was one of your tiny pearl buttons that was the VITAL CLUE, Nadia," I say. "It must have fallen off the present when Bradley was hiding it."

We are SO relieved – but also MYSTIFIED. WHY did he hide it? We see Bradley across the playground, still looking confident and smiling.

"Shall we say something?" asks Amy. "Tell the boys **we've won?**"

"And tell Bradley that we know it was *him*?" says Nadia.

But I say, "Bradley says he will find it tomorrow – let's see what he's planning first..."

EEK! I still don't have a costume for Egypt Day! Luckily I have some black card, enough for one pair of Anubis ears for me and a smaller pair for McClusky.

I put Mr D's present on my bedside table. There is

NO
WAY

I am letting it out of my sight.

An idea is beginning to take shape
in my head . . .

I think I've guessed what Bradley is up
to, but I'm one step ahead of him.

Ha HA!

I know just what to do.

Friday

Me and McClusky put on our **Anubis ears** and we all set off.

Arriving at school to see all our class dressed up and looking

FANTASTIC!

There are two sphinxes, a hippo, *three* Cleopatras – Amy, Alisha and Frankie – and *somebody* is disguised as the **Curse of the Mummy,** shuffling along trailing grubby bandages ...

His face is covered and he doesn't speak, only groans, but his great height and birthday rosette make it pretty obvious who it is!

Joe has borrowed his mum's eyeliner.
"Egyptian boys wore make-up too,
you know!" he says, and he shows us
how to use it perfectly.

Instead of going to our classroom, we gather in the hall.

Mrs Bagshott the head teacher comes in to admire our **Ancient Egypt** display.

"How splendid! WELL DONE!" she says.

We stand **proudly** next to our work and she takes our photograph.

! ! ! ! ! ! ! ! !

At that moment, Bradley steps
forward. He makes a big show of
lifting the pyramid, just as I expected.
But of course the present

ISN'T
THERE!

Bradley looks panicked
and horrified.
His **TA-DA** moment
has come to nothing.

I take the present out from under
my jumper and give it to Mr D.
He is absolutely **over the moon**.

"I LOVE IT! THANK YOU, guys!
You are *the best*!"

The girls' team high five each other.
The rest of the boys' team are so
pleased to see Mr D so happy that
they don't seem to care that we won
and they lost, and they high five each
other too! The whole
class sings
"Happy Birthday".

While everyone is distracted,
I confront Bradley.

"It was **YOU** all along!" I say.

Bradley just shrugs and turns to walk away.

I carry on, **feeling cross**.

"You hid the present and then lied to us and pretended to *find* it yourself.

But WHY?"

He still doesn't answer, but he looks really upset.

"*Why*, Bradley?" I ask again, a bit more quietly this time.

"I thought people would like me if I was the **HERO** who saved the day," he says.

Now he looks so upset I think he might cry.

"You **won't** tell mr D,

will you?"

I wonder if his confidence is mostly **pretend** and whether he has any proper friends. I decide to let sleeping dogs lie, which means leaving things as they are and not stirring up trouble.

I have a

GENIUS

idea.

When I tell Bradley, he thinks
it is **genius** too!

While Mr D is busy handing
out **mummy jelly sweets**,
I lend Bradley my second-best
glittery pen and he adds a message
to Mr D's present.

Happy birthday, Mr D!
I LOVE my new class.
From Bradley ☺

"Bradley," I say, "would you like to come to my party on Sunday?"

Me and Beans sit together at lunch.
I tell him all about how my team
solved the case and he is
EXTREMELY impressed.

"I like it best when you and me are a
team, though," I say.

"ME TOO!" says Beans. "I only
joined in with Bradley because he
seemed lonely."

I am so glad we are **BEST FRIENDS**
again.

"See you on Sunday at your party!"
all my friends are saying to me.

"Can't wait to know what the surprise
is!"

"Neither can I!"

I think to myself.

SATURDAY

I am

waiting

 waiting

 waiting...

I still don't know ANYTHING about my birthday party.

Mum says, "Mum's the word!" and laughs a lot at her own joke.

134

But it's no laughing matter – everyone will be arriving *tomorrow* at three o'clock, expecting a **fantastic surprise**: and no one will be more surprised than **me!**

Me and the twins are banished from the kitchen.

Mum tells the twins to **plump** up the cushions in the sitting room, and tells me to tidy McClusky's corner.

At bathtime Mum insists that
McClusky has a bath too.

I give him an
extra brushing,
but he is *so* **wriggly**.
Why is he **SO** excited?

Snuggled down in bed, SO impatient for my birthday to arrive.

I bet I will be awake

ALL NIGHT.

Sunday

I open my eyes.

Happy birthday to ME!

The kitchen looks brilliant with dotty balloons, birthday garlands and bunting everywhere. Mum is up already, having a cup of tea.

While she is giving me a big hug, McClusky and the twins come bowling in like a *tornado*.

Time to OPEN my presents!

The twins give me *FRED AND FLO'S FANTASTICALLY FAB STORYBOOK*, McClusky gives me some Dalmatian stickers and Mum gives me a pair of new red trainers – *exactly* the ones I was hoping for.

And *at last* it's time for my

PARTY!

As they arrive, each guest is given a colourful ticket that says ADMIT ONE, and they go through a red velvet curtain into the sitting room.

Dot's birthday surprise
★ ★ ★ ★ ★
ADMIT ONE

Inside it is **very dark**, lit only with fairy lights around the room.

There are rows of comfy chairs and cushions on the floor.

Mum has transformed our sitting room into a

cinema!

She is giving out popcorn in dotty card holders from the popcorn machine borrowed from school (so *that* was the big object under the sheet!).

We watch my new top-favourite **scary movie,** which is *Zombie Graveyard Ghouls.*

"Ha ha, Bradley," I say, "did you think it would be a *princess flower-fairy* sort of film?" I nudge him jokily and he laughs.

When we have **screamed** halfway through, McClusky comes in with a basket of ice creams. He is wearing a gold usherette's hat Mum has made for him (so *that's* why he had a little piece of gold thread on his ear!).

When it's finished, the BIGGEST surprise is Laura saying, "That was the best film I have *ever* seen."

We play a few rounds of **Wink Murder** and **Who Am I?**, then a delicious party tea is delivered from Pink Vanilla, which is my very favourite café.

And best of all...

Mum has made me *exactly* the birthday cake I wanted!

This has been the **best birthday EVER.**

Thank you SO MUCH, Mum!

The case of Mr D's **missing birthday present** – solved.

What will our next tricky mystery be?

Have you read?

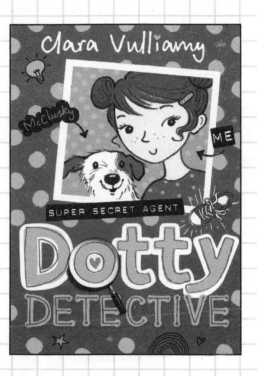

When someone seems set on sabotaging the school show, Dot is determined to find out how, and save the day!

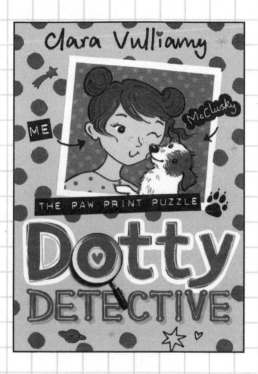

When Dot starts hearing strange noises at night, Beans is convinced there has to be something SPOOKY afoot. But, before they can be certain, Dot and Beans must GET PROOF.

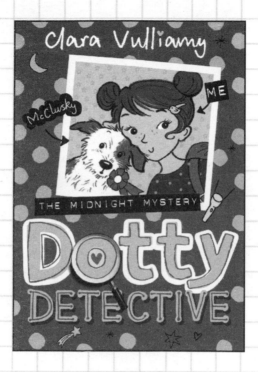

Dot and Beans can't wait for their school trip to Adventure Camp where they will do lots of exciting adventure activities and may even win the Adventurers' Prize! But why is someone trying to spoil the fun?

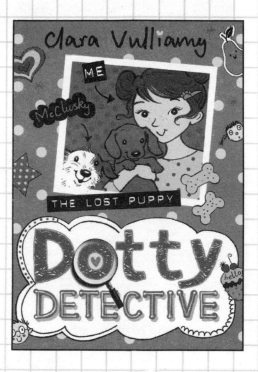

There's a fantastic surprise at the school gates – Dot's friend Joe has brought along his new sausage dog puppy, Chipolata! She is SOOOOOO cute! But then she goes missing. Can the Join the Dots Detectives track down the lost little dog?

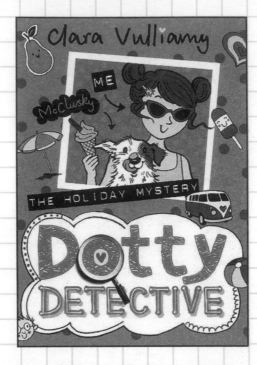

Join the gang on their next adventure as
Dot and her best friend, Beans, set off on
holiday. There are so many fun things to
do on the beach and at the campsite, but
eating doughnuts at the Nook café is their
favourite! So when things start mysteriously
disappearing from the Nook the Join the Dots
Detectives are determined to solve the case!

Join Dot, Beans and McClusky
on their next case…

LOOK OUT FOR ANOTHER

Dotty DETECTIVE

coming soon…